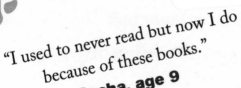

"I used to never read but now I do because of these books."
Sasha, age 9

"I love that the friends go on cool adventures that are always good for the Earth."
Desmond, age 7

"I wish I could be the new member of the Playdate Adventure Club."
Freya, age 9

"I like how the friends care about the Earth and water."
Audrey, age 7

Katy

Chatty, sociable and kind. She's the glue that holds the Playdate Adventure Club together. Likes animals (especially cats) and has big dreams of saving the world one day.

Cassie

Shy but brave when she needs to be. She relies on her friends to give her confidence. Loves dancing, especially street dance, but only in the privacy of her bedroom.

Zia

Loud, confident and intrepid. She's a born leader but can sometimes get carried away. Likes schoolwork and wants to be a scientist when she's older, just like her mum.

Luca

The newest member of the club. He's shy, like his cousin Cassie, but not when it comes to going on an adventure. Is obsessed with watching nature programmes.

Thunder

Big, white and fluffy with grey ears, paws and tail. He's blind in one eye, but that's what makes him extra special. Likes chasing mice, climbing trees and going on adventures. Is also a cat.

**Join the friends on
all their Playdate Adventures**

THE GREAT SAFARI RESCUE

Book Five

THE GREAT SAFARI

RESCUE

Emma Beswetherick

Illustrated by Anna Woodbine

ROCK THE BOAT

A Rock the Boat Book

First published by Rock the Boat,
an imprint of Oneworld Publications, 2022

ISBN 978-0-86154-236-9 (paperback)
ISBN 978-0-86154-237-6 (ebook)

Printed and bound in Great Britain by Clays Ltd, Elcograf S.p.A.

Oneworld Publications
10 Bloomsbury Street, London, WC1B 3SR, England

Stay up to date with the latest books,
special offers, and exclusive content from
Rock the Boat with our newsletter

Sign up on our website
oneworld-publications.com/rtb

To my husband and kids,
because we'll never forget
our treasured safari adventure

CHAPTER ONE

"Thunder, *please* keep still," Katy begged, as she wrestled a large, fidgety cat onto her lap. "Only a few more drops, then your eye will be as good as new." She spoke calmly, holding his eyelid open with her left hand while squeezing in the drops with her right. As soon as the liquid touched his eye, his claws dug into her legs and he launched himself onto the floor.

"You only make it harder for yourself, you know," Katy said, as Thunder glared at her from the corner of her bedroom.

Thunder was Katy's one-eyed rescue cat and absolute best friend in the world, apart from Cassandra and Zia. For the past two weeks he'd had an eye infection in his working eye, but the vet had said he was finally on the mend.

Thunder hated going to the vet, but Katy loved it. Vet Akoojee had some incredible stories from his time working with the "big five" safari animals – lions, leopards, elephants, rhinos and buffalos. Wow – treating dogs and cats looked like fun, but working with wild animals in the African savannah? That sounded unbelievably cool!

Katy was just putting Thunder's eye drops back in the fridge when the doorbell rang.

"I'll get it!" Katy called.

"Not if I get there first!" her dad teased.

Katy slammed the fridge door shut and sprinted past him on the landing. Her friends

2

had arrived for a playdate, along with Cassandra's cousin, Luca. Katy was excited to see Luca, but she was a bit worried that having him there might change how they played today. More than anything, she just hoped the magic of the Playdate Adventure Club would still work.

She ran down the stairs from their upper-floor flat, then swung open the front door with a wide smile. "Hi, Cassie! Hi, Zia! Hi, Luca!"

Her two best friends were standing on the doorstep, beaming right back at her. But Luca hovered behind his cousin, looking a bit lost.

"Good to see you all," said Katy's dad, appearing behind her in the narrow hallway. "Come on up."

Cassandra and Zia waved goodbye to Cassandra's mum, then hurried inside, flinging off their shoes and coats before dashing upstairs. Katy showed Luca in and they headed up too.

"I'm happy for them to stay for a few hours. They're no trouble," Katy heard her dad say. But she didn't wait to hear Cassandra's mum's reply. Her friends were already in her bedroom, clearly as eager to begin their playdate as she was.

Luca followed her into the room, and Katy walked over to Thunder, who was still sulking in the corner.

4

"Thunder, meet Luca," she said, scooping the enormous white cat into her arms and nuzzling his soft grey head.

"He's so fluffy!" Luca exclaimed. "Can I s-stroke him?"

"Of course, he's very friendly. Although he's just come back from the vet, so he's a bit grumpier than usual."

Once Luca had finished fussing over Katy's cat, Cassandra and Zia had a turn. Thunder meowed, cheering up with all the attention.

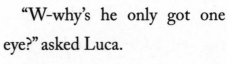

"W-why's he only got one eye?" asked Luca.

"He lost one in a fight with another cat before he was rescued," Zia said proudly, before Katy had even opened her mouth to reply.

"It's what makes him extra special," added Cassandra. "Right, Katy?"

"Right. The most extra-special ragdoll cat ever!" Katy plopped Thunder back on the floor. It was obvious her friends loved him as much as she did. *Almost.* "Glad you could come, Luca. Are you enjoying being in our class?"

"It's, er, O*K*, I s-suppose." Luca's dark eyes gazed down at the floor. "I mean, you guys are g-great and everything. And it's fun seeing more of my c-cousin." He glanced up at Cassandra, who placed a hand on his shoulder.

6

"But I miss my old friends. I s-speak to them online, but it's not the same as seeing them every day."

Luca used to live in another part of the country, but his mum had recently got a new job, which meant the whole family had had to move. He had a stammer and Cassandra had told them it made speaking a challenge for him. Katy couldn't imagine what it must feel like not to be able to get all her words out easily. She was determined to try to include him, especially because she knew what it felt like to be the new kid at school.

"Well, you can play with us any time," Katy said.

"Absolutely!" Cassandra and Zia agreed.

"Hey, you'll never guess where Thunder's vet worked before." Katy hoped this might get Luca talking. Cassandra had mentioned he was really into nature programmes.

"He used to care for wild animals in South Africa!"

"That's awesome," said Luca. "I've always w-wanted to go on safari. I watched a d-documentary about lions in Kruger National Park once. That's one of the h-huge g-game reserves in South Africa."

"That's where Vet Akoojee worked!" Katy exclaimed.

"Hey, maybe that's where we could go on our next adventure?" Zia suggested excitedly.

Cassandra fiddled nervously with her hair clips. "I don't know, Zia. It's cool seeing lions on TV, but would you want to come face to face with one in real life?"

"I w-would," said Luca.

"And me," Katy agreed. Thunder started meowing and pawing at her legs. "I think Thunder would love it too!" She giggled.

8

"But I know what you mean, Cassie. It could be scary out in the wild. We'd all be together, though. There's safety in numbers, remember?"

"*S-safety in numbers?*" echoed Luca. "We're not actually g-going to South Africa, though, are we? I mean, we're only saying that we'd *like* to g-go there. Not that we *are*."

Katy looked at her friends and they nodded. It was time to tell Luca about what *really* happened on their playdates.

"Go on, Cassie," Katy encouraged. "He's your cousin."

"OK…" Cassandra stopped fiddling with her hair clips and took Luca's hands in her own. "Can you promise to keep a secret?"

9

CHAPTER TWO

"I *p-promise*!" Luca let go of his cousin's hands and put his right palm in the air.

"Cross your heart?" Cassandra asked.

"Hope to die?" Zia added.

"Stick a needle in your eye?" Katy joined in.

"Put a cupcake on your tie?" finished Cassandra, giggling.

"Yes, yes," cried Luca. "All those things!"

Cassandra took a deep breath. "OK, so on our first playdate, Katy, Zia and I formed a secret club called the Playdate Adventure Club.

Thunder's also a member and, after today, you will be too."

"A s-secret club sounds kinda cool!" Luca smiled.

"Yes, but this secret club is also *kinda* special," echoed Katy.

"You see," said Cassandra, "in our secret club, you don't just imagine an adventure, you actually go on one."

Luca stared at his cousin blankly.

"What Cassie's trying to say," Zia chipped in, "is that we close our eyes and picture ourselves on an adventure and when we open our eyes, we're transported anywhere we wish to go. So far we've been to a far-off galaxy, the North Pole, the Atlantic Ocean and an enchanted forest."

"And this time," Katy said, "we're off to South Africa!"

Luca's mouth fell open. "You mean, we're really g-going on safari? Today? Like, right n-now?"

The girls nodded, but they could see from Luca's expression he was struggling to believe it.

"First, we need to start planning," said Zia. "How should we get there?"

"Most people drive jeeps on safari," said Katy. "Would that work?"

"Brilliant!" Cassandra cried. "Remember when we built a rocket out of recycling to fly us to the Wishing Star? This time, why don't we build a *flying* safari jeep?"

"We *could*, if the recycling hadn't been picked up this morning," Katy sighed.

The girls searched the room for anything else they could use.

13

"Look!" Katy grabbed four scatter cushions covered in metallic sequins from her bed. "These could be the wheels."

"How about this for the steering wheel?" said Cassandra, taking a large circular lid off a tin used to store hairbands.

"And this for the g-gear stick?" suggested Luca, picking up a hairbrush from the dressing table.

"Nice one, Luca!" said Cassandra.

Everyone got to work. Katy asked Luca to help her bring in four leather chairs from the kitchen, which they arranged like the seats in a car, two in front and two behind. Thunder jumped onto one of the chairs and started to lick his paw.

Next, Katy leaned the four round cushions against the chairs, then they all helped carry her dressing table over to double as a bonnet and dashboard. Cassandra added the steering wheel and Luca the gear stick. For the boot, they dragged over a toy chest. Finally, they used the lid to trap two of Katy's colourful skirts, so they fanned out like wings on either side.

The friends stood back, admiring their creation.

"Well, I think it's great!" Katy smiled.

"I do t-too," agreed Luca.

"And me!" said Cassandra. "Zia? How about you?"

"I *like* it… But I think it's missing something."

They all fell silent, wondering what the something could be.

"I know!" said Luca. "In the d-documentary, there was this super cool jeep with a t-tent attached to the roof. The t-tent could open out so the people driving had somewhere safe off the ground to stay each night. P-perhaps we could add something like that?"

"That would finish it off perfectly!" Cassandra clapped her hands, happy that her cousin was getting involved. She hadn't seen him this enthusiastic about anything since he'd moved here. "Katy, do you still have that pop-up play tent?"

"You mean this?" Katy dragged a large camouflage bag from under her bed.

"Yes!" Luca cried, as she pulled the tent out of its bag. It sprang into shape and Luca helped her secure it above the chairs.

Zia was still staring at their make-believe jeep. "How about we try to make it more environmentally friendly?" She walked over to the dressing table and laid the three-panelled mirror flat, so it was facing the ceiling.

"These could be solar panels, so the jeep is powered by sunlight!"

"B-brilliant!" Luca exclaimed.

"Now it's definitely finished!" Cassandra beamed.

"Just one more thing," said Katy. "We should pack a few bits before we go. Remember how useful our backpacks were in the North Pole?"

She grabbed her backpack from the cupboard and started throwing things inside from the toy chest – a camera, a compass, a dress-up vet's kit. Then she ran to the kitchen to fill some water bottles, before sprinting back into her bedroom and tossing the last few items into her bag. "Now, who's ready to go on an adventure?"

"Luca, over here," said Cassandra.

The four friends formed a circle next to the jeep. Thunder looked up curiously from his chair.

"So, Luca," said Katy, "you need to close your eyes and imagine flying out of this bedroom and travelling thousands of miles to the hot African savannah. Can you do that?"

Luca squeezed his eyes shut and Katy could tell he was forming a picture in his mind.

"I've g-got it!" he whispered.

"Great! Now, everyone, hold hands. Then close your eyes and repeat after me: I wish to go on an adventure!"

"*I wish to go on an adventure*," they all chanted.

Katy hadn't felt this nervous-cited since their first adventure to the Wishing Star. She hoped more than ever before that their wish was about to come true.

CHAPTER THREE

"Nothing seems to be happening," said Katy, risking a quick peek.

"Luca," Zia whispered. "You've got to keep hold of my hand!"

"S-sorry," he said. "It felt t-tingly. I d-didn't mean to let go."

Katy waited for Luca to join the circle back together. "OK, I think we need to say the words again."

"*I wish to go on an adventure!*" they repeated.

This time, they all started to experience a

familiar sparkling sensation shooting around their bodies. Familiar to the girls, anyway. Luca froze as his body went hot then cold then fizzy then bubbly, all in the space of a few seconds.

Only when their bodies had returned to normal did they dare open their eyes.

"OH," squealed Katy.

"MY," shrieked Zia.

"GOODNESS!" shouted Cassandra.

"U-UNBELIEVABLE!" Luca staggered backwards in a daze.

Their makeshift jeep was now magically transformed into a real safari jeep, hovering above the floor. It had dark cream side panels, giant black wheels with metallic hubcaps, three solar panels on the bonnet and a huge iron bumper on the front. There were no windows – making it perfect for "big five" spotting

– just a metal frame supporting a roof wit.
camouflage tent fastened on top.

"Am I seeing things, or is that the sky?"
Katy screamed, looking up towards her ceiling,
which had completely disappeared!

Luca rubbed his eyes. "When you said the
P-Playdate Adventure Club was special, I didn't
totally believe you. B-but I do now. Either that,
or I'm having a very weird dream."

"It's no dream," Cassandra assured him.

"This is as real as it gets," said Zia. "Have
you seen what we're wearing?"

Luca looked down to find his clothes had
been transformed into full safari gear – khaki
shorts, a gilet, walking boots with white socks
and a pair of binoculars round his neck.

"So, are we ready?" asked Katy, breaking the
silence.

"Yes!" the others chorused.

Zia flicked her plait to one side and strode over to the driver's door. "Is everyone happy if I drive? I mean, fly?"

Katy and Cassandra exchanged a smile. An adventure wouldn't be the same without Zia's confidence.

"Be careful, it's quite a step up," Zia continued, hauling herself into the driver's seat.

Katy and Cassandra were about to follow when they noticed that Luca looked a bit shaky.

"Don't worry, Zia's a pro," Katy said. "She flew our rocket brilliantly."

"Are you all right?" Cassandra put her arm round her cousin's shoulders. "You know, when we flew to the Wishing Star, I didn't want to go at first. And when a waterslide appeared out of Katy's window, I was terrified of letting go of the sides. I still get butterflies in my tummy before our adventures, but I promise you're going to love it!"

"I s-suppose I've always wanted to go on a proper adventure. B-but this—" Luca gestured at the hovering jeep – "is pretty insane!" He walked up to it.

"Does that mean you're coming?" asked Cassandra.

"Only if I can b-bagsy the front!" he shouted,

25

racing round to the passenger seat.

Cassandra hopped in the back, while Katy threw the backpack into the boot then clambered into the seat beside her. Straight away, Thunder climbed onto Katy's lap and started kneading her legs with his front paws.

"Thunder! Have you been here the whole time?" she said. "Hey, cool cap and neck scarf!" Thunder flumped down and gazed at her sulkily. "I don't think Thunder's in the mood for conversation today!" She giggled.

"Ready?" Zia asked.

"READY!" her friends shouted.

"Then let's go on safari!" Zia turned the key in the ignition and the jeep started to rise further off the floor.

"Look!" Katy cried, as two large, stripy bat-like wings fanned out on each side.

"Wow – c-cool wings!" said Luca.

26

Zia hit a button that said "SAFARI" in big letters and pressed down on the accelerator. Before they could even draw breath, they were shooting out of the bedroom and up into the sky. The world below grew smaller and smaller. The houses shrank to matchboxes, with ant-size cars moving along spaghetti-like roads.

Within moments, they were whizzing through the clouds, speeding towards the great continent of Africa.

CHAPTER FOUR

Time seemed to stretch and squeeze as they flew. They could have been in the air for hours or minutes, it was impossible to tell.

"I love being above the clouds," said Cassandra dreamily. "I've always imagined another world up here."

"Me too," said Katy. "It'd have a candyfloss castle with turrets made from lollipops."

"Hey," called Zia, noticing the "SAFARI" button had begun to flash. "I think we're almost there!"

The jeep began its descent, but as it broke through the last of the thinning clouds, Luca spotted a pink shape hurtling towards them. Then another and another...

"Z-Zia, look out!" he shouted.

Zia yanked the steering wheel and they swerved to the left, just in time to avoid a flock of flamingos.

"Woah! Look how pink they are!" Katy exclaimed. "Good job, Zia!"

"I think I'm going to be sick," whimpered Cassandra.

"Hold on, cuz, we'll be l-landing soon," said Luca.

They could see the ground clearly now – a vast expanse of sandy-coloured earth with black dots moving around. As the jeep descended, the dots grew bigger, until they could make out the shapes of animals. Some were moving in herds and small packs, others were roaming alone.

"Look, a giraffe!" cried Katy, peering through her binoculars. "I've always dreamed of seeing one in the wild!"

"And over there! Is that a rhino?" shrieked Zia.

Thunder put his paws up on the side of the jeep so he could have a better view. Cassandra's eyes were fixed firmly on her lap.

"Cassie, it helps to look forward if you're feeling sick." Katy squeezed her hand.

"How about you, Luca?" asked Zia. "All good?"

"Couldn't be better. Wow, I think that's a l-leopard. There – u-under that tree!"

31

Zia scanned the ground for a safe place to land. "Hold on!" she shouted.

The engine's roar softened to a gentle purr, the wings retracted, then the wheels slammed into the ground, sending up clouds of red dust. The jeep bounced once, twice, rolling forwards a few more metres before coming to a sudden stop. Thunder was flung off the seat and landed at Katy's feet with a yowl.

"We're here! Kruger National Park!" Zia announced, rubbing her neck. "I think I need to practise my landings!"

She turned off the engine and they were hit by the intense, stifling heat of the day. The sky was the bluest of blue and GIGANTIC. The red earth was cracked and parched. Large thorny bushes grew in clusters, and straight ahead was the strangest-looking tree they had ever seen. The trunk was huge and twisted, with branches that looked like roots growing up into the sky.

"That's a b-baobab," Luca pointed out. "Otherwise known as the upside-d-down tree, or the tree of life. It can live for thousands of years."

"It looks fun to climb," said Thunder, breaking his silence.

"Who s-said that?" Luca whipped his head round.

"I forgot to tell you," Katy giggled, relieved that Thunder had finally cheered up. "Thunder can talk on our adventures! Can't you, Thunder?" She pulled him in for a cuddle and started kissing his cheeks.

"Of course I can talk. All the animals on our adventures can!" Thunder replied, wriggling out of Katy's arms to escape her kisses.

Everyone laughed as he wiped his face with his paw.

"That's one c-cool cat," said Luca.

"At your service," answered Thunder, raising his cap.

They were about to get out of the jeep when there was a deafening roar. A magnificent male lion stepped out from behind the baobab and prowled towards them. Thunder burrowed back into Katy's arms, keeping his one eye glued to the big cat's every move.

"Everyone, duck!" Zia whispered urgently.

Nobody dared breathe as the lion began to circle the jeep. It stopped every few paces to lick its front right paw.

"I think he's hurt," Katy said, peeping from the window.

"Get down!" whispered Cassandra, trembling with fear.

"D-don't worry, he can only see us if we h-hang our heads out of the jeep and wave our

34

arms around," said Luca. "At the moment, he probably thinks we're a big r-rock or something. I learned that in the documentary. He won't attack unless we p-provoke him."

Katy could hear her heart pounding as the lion started to circle their vehicle. He was huge and muscular, with piercing eyes and terrifyingly sharp teeth. Finally, he seemed bored of the jeep, licking his paw one more time before limping off into the bushes.

Cassandra let out a gasp of air. "Phew, that was close!"

"Incredible," said Thunder. "To think that *I'm* related to *him*."

Zia loosened her sweaty hands on the steering wheel. "OK, time to see what else we can find." She started up the engine. "And keep your eyes peeled. We don't want to become the next lion's dinner!"

They set off again, the jeep bouncing along the bumpy ground. The anticipation of seeing a wild animal was almost as exciting as coming face to face with one.

They spotted drifting herds of wildebeests and zebras, a grumpy-looking warthog shuffling alongside an even grumpier-looking baby, four giraffes flopping in the shade of some trees and a huge African buffalo swaying gently on its legs. Cassandra pointed out a turquoise bird with colourful wing tips and a purple tummy.

"That's a l-lilac-breasted roller. They do funny m-mating dances in the air," said Luca, peering through his binoculars. "But that one doesn't look so well. In fact," he continued, raising his voice so the others could hear, "h-have you noticed that *all* the animals seem to be acting s-strangely?" Katy nodded, but the other two shook their heads. "I know it's super hot, but

37

they look so w-weak and tired. I reckon the animals are d-dehydrated."

"What does that mean?" asked Cassandra, proud that her cousin was talking so much. She knew he didn't find it easy.

"It means they're really thirsty and need water *soon*," said Katy.

"Perhaps they're in the middle of a drought?" suggested Zia.

"I think you're—" Luca suddenly broke off, distracted by a large grey shape in the bushes up ahead. "Zia, s-stop!" he shouted, wanting to get a closer look.

Zia hit the brake, making them all lurch forwards.

Taking cover in the undergrowth was a young elephant, a little bigger than the lion. Its trunk was drooping towards the ground.

"Hi there," said Katy gently, leaning her head out of the jeep. But the elephant retreated further into the thorny bushes. "We're not here to hurt you. We're friends, see," she continued. "Your home is brilliant, but all the animals look sad. Is everything OK?"

The elephant took a cautious step forward. "You haven't come at a good time," it sighed. "But my older brothers and sisters think I'm too small to help. That's why I'm hiding. I've argued with them and—"

A trumpeting sound in the distance stopped the elephant in its tracks and it vanished back into the bushes. Moments later, hundreds of animals came stampeding out of nowhere, charging full throttle in the direction of the noise.

39

CHAPTER FIVE

"What's going on?" said Katy, still staring at the spot where the young elephant had been.

"There's one way to find out!" Zia pressed down on the accelerator. Up ahead was a dusty cloud where hooves and paws had recently trampled, and the friends could hear the elephants trumpeting in the distance.

They followed the dust and the noise, swinging in and out of bushes and bumping up and down ditches, until they spotted a crowd of animals up ahead. Zia parked the jeep so they were camouflaged behind a thorny bush.

From their hiding place, they could see that the animals were standing round a huge crater. On one side was a large elephant with her herd.

"That must be the m-matriarch or m-mummy elephant," whispered Luca.

The rest of the animals – lions, leopards, cheetahs, hyenas and wild dogs, along with giraffes, zebras, rhinos and every breed of antelope – were gathered round the crater's edge. They were shouting and growling, jostling and pushing to get to the front. Every now and again, the friends caught words like "water", "thirst" and "drought".

"Look, there's the elephant from earlier," Zia whispered, pressing her nose against the windscreen.

The young elephant was close to their

42

hide-out, trying desperately to get the attention of the other animals. But it wasn't having much luck. The trumpeting sound that came out of its little trunk couldn't compete with the thunderous clamour. Eventually, it gave up.

"Wait here," said Katy, swinging open her door and jumping to the ground.

"What are you doing?" Cassandra called softly, eyeing the noisy group of animals. "*Please* stay in the jeep – there's a whole pride of lions out there!"

"I just want to speak to the elephant and see if we can help in any way," Katy whispered. "I don't mind going alone." But even as she said it, Zia jumped out too.

"Not you as well, Zia!" Cassandra said. Then Luca hopped out, followed by Thunder. "You can't *all* go without me," she sighed, clambering out after them.

43

Katy ran up and threw her arms round Cassandra's shoulders. "Thank you," she said. "The Playdate Adventure Club always sticks together, right?"

"Right," said Cassandra, clipping her sweaty fringe off her forehead. "Safety in numbers."

Keeping low to the ground, they crept towards the young elephant. Luckily, the rest of the animals were so busy squabbling, it was easy to move unnoticed. Soon they were only a few metres away, hidden behind a towering termite mound.

"Psst!" Katy called, trying to get the elephant's attention.

"Louder," urged Luca.

"PSSSSSTTTT!" she called again.

The elephant turned its head.

"Over here!" Katy leaned out from behind the mound and beckoned the elephant over.

46

It glanced around to check she hadn't meant a different animal, then plodded towards her.

"Hey, you followed me!" it said, frowning. "What are you doing here?"

"That's what *we* want to know," said Katy. "We didn't get a chance to introduce ourselves before. I'm Katy. These are my friends, Cassie, Zia and Luca – and this is Thunder. He's my pet cat."

"Nice to meet you," said Thunder. "We animals need to stick together! And what's *your* name?"

"I'm Izwi. It's Zulu for 'voice'. It's one of the

reasons my brothers and sisters laugh at me." Izwi hung his head, swishing his trunk along the dusty ground.

"They say my voice is too small and I need a new name."

"*No* voice is too small to be heard," said Katy. She put her hand on the elephant's back, which felt rough and warm. "And *no* creature is too small to stand tall. Perhaps you can find another way to make them listen."

"What *is* it you're trying to say, anyway?" asked Cassandra.

Izwi stopped swinging his trunk and eyed the strange gang. "You said we all look sad. You're right – we *are* sad. We're in the middle of a drought, you see. All the watering holes have dried up. Except for this one here." Izwi pointed his trunk towards the crater. In the middle, the friends could make out a shallow pool of water.

"Mama Elephant discovered it. She called the rest of the animals here to drink. But it's drying up fast. Soon this one will have disappeared like the others. That's why the animals are arguing. They're fighting over the last drops of water, when what we really need to do is work out how to get *more*."

"Is that what you wanted to s-say?" asked Luca. "Just now, when you were trying to get their attention?"

"Exactly. But nobody listens to me."

"*We're* listening," said Cassandra. "Look, I've always been scared about speaking out. I avoid standing up in class because it makes me feel sick. But my friends here – they've taught me that *true* friends stick by you. They look after you and cheer you on. If we promise to help find a solution, do you think you could find your voice?"

"You'd do that?" said Izwi in amazement. He took a long breath in and out, then

49

looked around, thinking. "OK, I've got an idea. Follow me!"

The friends stayed low to the ground as he led them past the animals and up to a rocky outcrop overhanging the watering hole. Izwi climbed to the very top where there was a cave hollowed into the rocks. He stepped inside and they crowded in next to him. Then he raised his trunk and blew with all his might.

BAHRUUUUUUUUUUUUUUHHHHHAA AAAAAA!

The noise echoed around the cave, bouncing off the walls. It was so loud the friends had to put their hands over their ears.

At once, everything went quiet outside.

"Now go and make them listen!" said Cassandra. "We're right behind you."

Izwi stepped cautiously into the sunlight. "Please, you have to stop arguing," he said, gazing down at the animals. Katy could see that his knees were trembling.

"Look, it's Izwi with the *small* voice!" jeered an elephant with a ragged ear from below.

"We can't hear you!" jested another and the group of elephants sniggered.

"They must be Izwi's brothers and sisters," whispered Zia. "Why do older siblings always think they know best?"

Izwi started to back away.

"You can *do* it," encouraged Katy.

The young elephant took another deep breath and raised his head into the air.

"We need more water," he said in a slow, clear voice. "But arguing isn't going to bring any back to our part of the savannah. We must call a truce between *all* the animals. Let's *share* ideas, not *fight* about them."

"But we don't have time," snarled a hyena.

"Have you seen the water disappearing while we've been standing here?" boomed a hippo. Its enormous mouth opened wide, bearing dangerously large teeth. Katy gasped – it was obvious why hippos were the deadliest animals in Africa.

"Exactly, we *don't* have much time," Izwi begged.

The animals started nodding their heads. A couple of Izwi's siblings muttered to each other but were nudged into silence by their elders.

"We need to come up with a plan – *together*!" Izwi continued. "And I have some new friends who want to help."

All the animals were listening now. They started to look around.

"Ready?" Izwi turned to face the gang.

Katy looked at her friends, still hiding in the shadows. "It's now or never," she said.

54

CHAPTER SIX

Thunder led the way, swaggering over to the edge of the ridge. *He's trying to impress the big cats*, Katy thought with a smile. *I'm not sure it's going to work!*

"Good afternoon," he said. "I'm Thunder and these are my friends. We'd like to help you." The crowd below stared in shock. They'd clearly never seen a pet cat before either. But as the children joined Thunder, the jeering started up again.

"Why should we listen to four humans and a small cat in a hat?" demanded the elephant with the ragged ear.

"Yeah," agreed a crocodile, snapping its jaws. "It's because of *humans* that we don't have enough water in the first place."

Katy wiped the sweat from her forehead. If that's how the animals felt, how were they were going to be able to do anything?

Luca was scratching his head, deep in thought.

"Look," he whispered, turning to the group. "D-drought has always been a part of life here. Every year there's a w-wet season and a dry season – it's a cycle, like our s-seasons back home. But *l–long* periods of drought are a result of climate change. Humans are d-definitely to blame for that, so you can see why the animals don't trust us."

"That's terrible," Cassandra said, feeling helpless.

The jeering was getting so loud now, the friends could hardly hear each other above the racket. Izwi pulled them closer together with his trunk. "You need to find a way to convince them that you really are here to help."

"Wait a moment!" Katy shouted, spotting the lion who'd circled their jeep. He was still licking his right paw. "Izwi, you stay here and keep the animals busy. The rest of you, come with me." Before they could ask any questions, she was off, scrambling down the rocky ridge.

Katy's friends caught up with her back at the jeep.

57

"W-what's going on?" Luca panted.

"I've thought of a way to get the animals to trust us," said Katy, swinging open the boot. "Remember that lion from earlier? The one with the injured paw? He's over there, with that pride of lions. If I can heal his paw, I'm sure the animals will see that we're good humans and not the kind that can't be trusted."

"But how are you going to get near the lions without being eaten?" Cassandra asked nervously.

"Yeah, Katy," said Zia. "It's way too risky."

Katy grabbed her backpack. "Look, the only thing these animals are interested in right now is water. We've got to give it a go!" She slammed the boot shut and strode off towards the watering hole.

Moving in single file, they edged past thick

58

bushes until they were only metres away from the lions.

Katy placed her bag on the floor and coughed once…twice…

The male lion turned and roared. Katy could feel his hot, stale breath on her face.

"You're hurt," she said, her hand shaking as she pointed at his right paw. "I…I think I can make it better."

"I don't need your help," he growled. "Go away."

Thunder bounded over and bravely stood between Katy and the lion. "Cat to cat," he said seriously, bowing to show the enormous beast his respect, "if Katy says she can fix your paw, I suggest you let her try. She's always looked after me. I *even* let her put medicine in my sore eye to make it better."

Even though you hate it, Katy thought.

59

The lion flopped to the floor and began licking his paw again. "You really think she can help?"

"I *know* she can," said Thunder. He winked at Katy with his one blue eye, which was looking a lot clearer.

"OK!" the lion bellowed, so all the animals could hear. "You fix my paw and maybe we won't eat you. Sound fair?"

Katy swallowed hard, giving a shaky thumbs up to her friends before crouching down and placing her bag on the ground. Then she gently lifted the lion's paw. Immediately, she noticed a long, deep cut across the pad. "Ouch – that looks nasty."

"It was hyenas. I found some water at the bottom of another watering hole – a long way from here. I was about to drink when a pack of them attacked me. That was a couple of days ago, but the pain has been getting worse."

Katy took out her water bottle and turned to Luca. "Can you pour some into my hands?" she asked, cupping her palms to make a bowl. Luca followed her instructions and Katy slowly offered her hands out to the lion. Instantly, he started lapping with his large tongue. It felt rough and tickly, but that's when she remembered what Vet Akoojee had told her. *Animals can smell fear, so you need to stay calm and act confidently. They will only relax if you relax.*

When the lion had finished drinking, Katy rummaged in her bag for her vet's kit, knowing from previous adventures that she would find exactly what she needed. Inside was a bandage and some antiseptic cream.

"This may sting a little," she said, squeezing some cream onto her fingers and rubbing it into the lion's paw. The lion roared and pulled it away.

Katy looked him in the eye and took hold of his paw once more. "The cream will soothe the pain and will also treat any infection in the cut." She finished rubbing it in, then wrapped the bandage round his paw, securing it with a safety pin. "There," she said. "It will soon start to feel better. Tomorrow, you can take the dressing off."

The lion stood up and when he put his weight on his bandaged paw, it was obvious how much easier he found it to walk. He nodded his great head in gratitude, then turned to the crowd of animals.

"Izwi's right," he said, smiling at the young elephant. "We should listen to what these humans have to say."

CHAPTER SEVEN

Katy could sense her friends right behind her as she stepped forward to address the crowd. She felt dizzy from the heat and queasy with nerves, so it was a relief to know she wasn't alone.

"When we're having a debate at school, our teacher chooses an adjudicator," she explained.

"What's an *ad-ju-di-ca-tor*?" asked a young waterbuck.

"It's the person who keeps order and listens to every side of an argument. Ms Coco says that the adjudicator gets to have the final say."

"I like that idea," said Izwi. "Who should it be?"

Katy put her hand on Izwi's shoulder. "*You're* the one who wanted everyone to discuss things together. *You* should be the one to take charge."

All the animals nodded, except for Izwi's older siblings, who continued to mutter to each other until the lion roared at them and they fell silent. Izwi climbed to the top of the rocky outcrop. He cleared his throat and raised his head high.

"This drought is the worst I've experienced." This time, his voice sounded as wise as a teacher's. "Until Mama Elephant found this watering hole today, we hadn't had a drink in days. But this one is shrinking too and will soon run dry. Somehow, we need a way to get more water."

The animals nodded as they took in what Izwi was saying.

"I'd like you all to suggest ideas that we can discuss *together*," Izwi continued. "Ideas that *no one* will laugh at." He darted his brothers and sisters a warning look. "And remember, a solution will only be found if we use our imaginations. Who wants to go first?"

A velvet monkey jumped up and down, waving his arms in the air. "We should do a rain dance!"

67

"Yes, yes, a rain dance!" chanted a band of baboons, thumping their big hands on the dusty ground.

"Let's dance now!" called a springbok, kicking out her back legs as she pranced round in a circle.

"But have you ever known a rain dance to work so quickly?" asked an impala.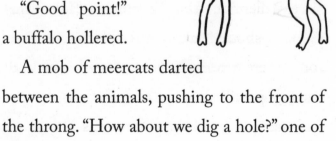

"Good point!" a buffalo hollered.

A mob of meercats darted between the animals, pushing to the front of the throng. "How about we dig a hole?" one of them said.

"A hole, a hole!" sang a honey badger. "These paws are made for digging. We'll find water for sure."

"We could suck the water up with our trunks," shouted an elephant.

"And shoot it back into the watering hole!" yelled another.

"I don't think you'll dig deep enough," mumbled an anteater.

A bat hawk swooped down from a nearby tree, landing on the back of a white rhino. "And what happens when the groundwater's used up?"

"Excellent question," hooted an eagle owl.

"We should leave this place and find somewhere *with* water," suggested a cheetah, pacing up and down impatiently.

A troupe of elderly wildebeests lifted their heads stiffly from the ground. "I'm afraid we don't have the strength for a journey," they groaned.

A long silence followed.

"Come on," encouraged Izwi. "Any more ideas?"

"You can have the water we brought with us," said Cassandra shyly. "I know it's not enough to go round…"

"That's very kind," said Izwi. "But it won't solve the problem. There must be some other way."

"You know, there's a lot of water in the sea," suggested an old crocodile. "What about drinking saltwater?"

"Saltwater isn't for drinking," scoffed an ostrich, puffing up her wings. "It'll only make us thirstier."

"But there must be *something* we can do?" whined a lion cub, clambering onto his mother's back.

More silence. Then: "There's always d-desalination," said Luca.

Everyone turned to stare at him, including his friends.

"Er...you know. Turning s-saltwater into fresh water?" he explained.

Not a peep, from anyone. They all looked puzzled.

Luca took a deep breath. "O-*K*... So if we use s-solar energy – that's energy from the sun – d-desalination is the most environmentally friendly way to make d-drinking water. If we fill the watering hole with s-saltwater, we could b-build something that takes out the s-salt and makes the water safe for d-drinking. I saw it on a survival documentary once." Luca sighed, as though relieved to have got to the end of such a long speech. But he looked proud of his explanation. *Yes!* thought Katy. *Go, Luca!*

The animals still looked confused.

"How do we *fill* the watering hole with saltwater?" mocked a wild dog. "We don't have saltwater in our part of Kruger."

"We could use the...er...the safari jeep!" Cassandra blurted, coming to her cousin's rescue. "We could fly to the sea and bring seawater back here." But then her shoulders drooped. "Except we don't have anything to collect the water in."

"How about the tent?" suggested Katy.

"Good idea!" cried Zia. "And if Izwi comes

too, he can suck the water up with his trunk!"

"That could work," replied Luca, thinking the plan through in his head. "I should stay behind to h-help. We're going to need a H-HUGE container to place in the watering hole – s-something to hold a large quantity of seawater. S-something like…" He looked around.

"There's a giant hollowed-out rock up here, next to the cave!" cried Izwi. "The elephants can help bring it down."

"P-perfect!" exclaimed Luca. He took another deep breath. "After we've f-filled it with seawater, we'll need something to put over it to t-trap the sun's heat."

"Could we use the tent again?" asked Zia. "It has windows on each side, a bit like a greenhouse. Would they heat up the water?"

"I'm sure that w-would work," Luca nodded.

"When the saltwater warms up, it will t-turn into water vapour. When the vapour hits the top of the tent and turns b-back into liquid, it will leave a layer of salt b-behind in the hollowed-out rock. The fresh water will d-drip down the insides into the surrounding watering hole. B-bingo!"

He picked up a twig and started sketching in the dust. When he'd finished his drawing, he added labels so everyone could see what they were trying to build.

"Zia, how about you collect seawater with Izwi and Katy?" suggested Cassandra. "I can stay here with Thunder to help Luca. How does that sound to you, Izwi?"

Izwi pointed his trunk towards the dried-up watering hole. "I think we've run out of time to come up with another plan. Let's go!"

CHAPTER EIGHT

"Are you sure I'm going to fit?" said Izwi, staring at the jeep.

"I'm more worried about it taking off!" joked Zia, trying her best to lighten the mood. "There should be room in the back."

The elephant tried to squeeze inside.

"Here, let us help," said Katy.

Together with Zia, she began to push. They pushed...and pushed. Still Izwi didn't budge. They were about to give up when – *POP!* – his big grey bottom suddenly shot from view and disappeared inside the jeep.

Phew, that was a close call, thought Katy, as she climbed into the front next to Zia. "Are you OK back there, Izwi?"

"Sure," Izwi answered, but Katy could tell he was squished.

"Which way to the sea?" said Zia, starting up the engine.

"That way!" Izwi cried, waving his trunk.

Zia swung the jeep round, then sped through a gap in the trees. Within seconds, the wings opened and they started rising slowly into the air. The engine strained under the weight of the elephant.

"Hold on tight!" Zia pressed on the accelerator to give the vehicle more power. The jeep juddered for a moment, and then shot up into the blue sky and across the open savannah.

Before long, Katy could make out the vast expanse of ocean in the distance. "I wonder how the others are getting on?" she thought out loud.

"I'm sure they'll be fine," Izwi said. "Elephants are brilliant at moving heavy objects. You know we have up to forty thousand muscles in our trunks?"

"Forty thousand?" Zia was impressed. "We only have six hundred in our entire bodies!"

"It's why trunks are so useful. They can suck up water *and* pick things up."

77

"That's amazing, Izwi!" Katy thought for a moment. "So, what are tusks for?"

"Moving things around," Izwi said proudly. "Stripping bark, gathering food. And for defence. Recently, the older elephants have even been using them to dig holes to find underground water. But they haven't had much luck. Hey, look!"

They were almost at the coast and the jeep began its descent. Zia gently pressed the brake and the wings started to retract.

"When we're steady above the water, I'll open up the tent and you can you start filling it, Izwi."

You make it sound so easy, thought Katy, hoping they could pull the plan off.

Zia brought the jeep down so it was hovering less than a metre over the sea, then she pressed the "TENT" button on the

78

control panel. Above them, they could hear the tent springing up from the roof. Katy leaned cautiously out of the passenger door and pulled herself up to take a look, gripping the metal frame for dear life. She didn't fancy another ocean adventure! She zipped up the tent door, leaving a narrow gap for Izwi's trunk to fit through.

"Now, Izwi!" she shouted.

Izwi leaned right out over the side of the jeep, keeping his back legs wedged under the seat. His trunk just reached the sea.

The elephant coughed and spluttered as he sucked up his first trunkful of saltwater. He sneezed, and all the water shot straight back out again. But he soon found his groove, sucking saltwater into his trunk, then twisting round so that he could reach up to the tent. Katy leaned out to help direct Izwi's trunk into the tent opening. It seemed to take forever, sucking and squirting, sucking and squirting. But at last, the tent was close to bursting.

"You can stop now, Izwi!" said Katy, closing the zip to keep the water from spilling.

"Do you think it's enough?" asked Izwi.

"Let's hope so!" said Zia. The jeep was so weighed down now she was worried about taking off again. With a choking sound, it lifted precariously into the air and extended its wings, tilting one way, then another.

"Watch out!" cried Katy, as a flock of pelicans came swooping towards them.

The large white birds circled the jeep, then pulled up close to the girls.

"Hi there!" said the pelican leading the flock. He was bigger than the others, with a yellow bill shaped like a bucket. "We've been watching you from the beach. We're curious – why have you filled your tent with seawater?"

"We're trying to save the last watering hole," said Zia.

"By turning saltwater into fresh water," added Katy.

"Then let us help you," said the pelican. The birds dived towards the sea, filling their bills

81

with water, before falling into a V-shape behind the jeep as it set off back to the watering hole.

Meanwhile, melting in the intense heat of the midday sun, Luca and Cassandra watched as four strong elephants heaved the enormous stone bowl into the middle of the crater, rolling it with their trunks. Thunder was riding on the back of the elephant with the ragged ear, shouting words of encouragement and helping them guide the bowl into place.

"W-where *are* they?" Luca muttered. "They should be back by now."

"They won't be long," Cassandra assured her cousin. "Zia and Katy don't know how to fail." *At least, I hope they don't*, she thought.

They stared up at the sky. At long last, a speck appeared in the distance.

"I think I see them!" Cassandra squealed.

82

The journey back had been much slower than the flight out. The extra weight of the water made the jeep sluggish and unstable. By the time Zia made a wobbly landing next to the watering hole, Katy felt as travel sick as Cassandra had earlier.

"Let's go!" shouted Thunder, waving his cap at the elephants.

They formed a line by the jeep and took turns to suck seawater from the tent and squirt it into the great depths of the stone bowl. The pelicans joined in too, tipping water from their bills until the bowl was filled to the brim.

"Hey, c-come and help with the tent," Luca instructed, beckoning his friends over.

They unfastened the tent from the groundsheet and lifted it off the jeep.

"We need to stretch the tent over the bowl so it forms a dome," Luca said, as they each took the end of a pole and pulled it into position.

"I can't reach that far!" cried Cassandra, struggling to pull her corner over the stone.

"Let me help," said Izwi. He tugged with his trunk until the fabric was fully stretched and Cassandra's pole was in place.

Finally, the tent was in position, the poles fixed into the parched ground. Now, when the saltwater evaporates, fresh water will drip back down the tent and into the watering hole.

All that was left to do was wait for the African sun to beat down on the tent windows, heating up the saltwater inside.

"I'm *so* thirsty," complained a young zebra. "Why's it taking so long?"

"Keep w-watching," said Luca, fingers and toes firmly crossed.

CHAPTER NINE

The animals were almost out of hope when at last it happened. Small beads of water began drip-drip-dripping from the bottom of the tent and drop-drop-dropping into the watering hole.

The drops turned into a trickle, then the trickle turned into a stream. Eventually, fresh water began to pour down the inside of the tent and into the watering hole. The friends watched as it transformed from a dusty crater into a miniature lake.

The animals stumbled down the banks and started to drink. There were cheers and trumpets and roars and brays of delight as they felt themselves and the wilderness around them coming back to life.

"We don't know how to thank you," Izwi shouted, laughing as a baby elephant squirted his back.

"It was a t-team effort!" Luca said. "And r-remember, you were the one who brought everyone together."

At that moment, Izwi's older brothers and sisters came plodding over.

"Hey, little bro," said the elephant with the ragged ear, ruffling Izwi's head with his trunk. "You've definitely lived up to your name. Izwi with the *big* voice. We're sorry we ever doubted you."

Izwi reached up and patted his brother's

back playfully in return. "You're forgiven," he said with a smile. "Just this once."

Katy turned to Luca. "So, how does it feel to be part of the Playdate Adventure Club?"

"And not just any member," added Zia, "but the one who came up with the plan to save the last watering hole."

Luca's face broke into a wide and happy grin. "It feels," he said, looking from his new friends to the animals playing in the water, "c-completely awesome."

Cassandra wrapped him in an enormous hug. "I'm proud of you, cuz!"

"What happens next?" asked the lion with the bandaged paw. "We've saved the watering hole for now, but what if it runs out of water again?"

89

"The humans have agreed to leave us their tent," said Izwi. "And the pelicans have offered to refill the bowl with seawater whenever it runs low. But this solution is only temporary. The only way to stop the water crisis for good is for humans to change their behaviour."

"And animals," Thunder added. "We all need to do our bit."

"And animals!" Izwi laughed. "We should drink when we're thirsty and share what we have."

"I promise to tell more people about water conservation," said Katy, scooping up Thunder and nuzzling his head.

"And me!" Zia threw her arm round Katy's shoulder. "Why don't we talk to our class about it? We could even do a mini project?"

"I'd love that," said Cassandra, joining in the group hug. "And I'm going to stop having baths. From now on, it's short showers for me."

"I'll remember to turn the t-tap off when I'm cleaning my teeth," said Luca.

"Yes!" Izwi nodded. "If everyone talks about water and does their bit to save it, hopefully we can turn things around. Just don't forget what causes these long droughts in the first place."

"You mean c-climate change?" asked Luca. "You're right – we must do *everything* we can to help save the planet."

Cassandra took hold of her cousin's hands. "We learned about climate change on our previous adventures. I wish you'd been with us. We'll tell you all about them when we get home."

"Talking of home," said Katy wistfully, "we'd better say goodbye." She always hated the part of their adventures when they had to leave their new friends. "I'm going to miss you, Izwi."

"I'll miss you too," the elephant replied, reaching down with his trunk to pick something up. "Here, I have something for you all."

Izwi offered each of them a tiny wooden elephant. Katy was given two, one for her and one for Thunder. "I carved them myself," he said, smiling. "They're gifts to remind you how precious water is for our survival. Thank you, for everything you've done."

A chorus of *thank yous* rose up from around the watering hole. When the noise died down, Katy turned to the others.

"It's time," she said, picturing her bedroom and her dad pottering about in the kitchen. "Now hold hands and repeat after me: I wish to go home."

"*I wish to go home,*" they all said together.

At once, they experienced that same bubbly, fizzy, hot and cold sensation they'd felt at the start of their adventure. Electricity seemed to shoot around their bodies, making the hairs on their arms stand on end. Gradually, they returned to normal. Only then did they open their eyes.

"We're back!" shrieked Katy, looking around her room. "And my ceiling's in one piece!"

"I c-can't believe that just happened," murmured Luca.

Thunder meowed, then padded over to the bed, stretching and yawning.

"My elephant!" cried Luca. "It's shrunk and it's solid gold!"

"Another charm! Look, we've been collecting them," said Cassandra, showing him her bracelet.

"We were given charms on our other adventures too," explained Zia.

"Here," said Katy, rummaging in her bedside table drawer. "I made this for you this morning."

"A wristband!" Luca grinned. "Thanks, Katy."

Once their charms were in place, the four friends began to dismantle the jeep. Katy smiled secretly to herself, noticing that her tent was nowhere to be seen.

"I feel bad," she said, dragging the toy chest back to its usual spot. "I've taken water for granted until now."

"Me too," Zia agreed, throwing the sequined cushions onto the bed. "But I won't anymore."

Katy waved her bracelet in the air. "To not wasting water."

"And to our next adventure," said Zia, holding her bracelet against Katy's.

Cassandra pulled Luca into the circle. "To the newest member of our club!"

"And to new friends!" Luca beamed.

Katy looked around for the fifth member of the crew and spotted Thunder curled up under her bed, his eye closed. She gently fastened the charm to his collar, careful not to disturb him. But Thunder was already back in the wilds of South Africa, dreaming of lions.

95

How to Plan Your Own
Playdate Adventure

1. Decide where you would like to go on your adventure.

2. Plan how you would get there. Do you need to build anything or imagine yourself in a new land?

3. Imagine what exciting or challenging things might happen on your adventure.

4. Decide if you are going to learn anything from your adventure.

5. Most important of all, remember to have fun!

WATER

Did you know…?

Less than 3% of the water on Earth is freshwater that is drinkable. Of that, only about 1% is accessible in rivers, lakes, streams and waterholes. The rest is contained in glaciers and snowfields.

All living creatures need water to survive. However, the length of time animals can live without it varies. Take a look at these examples:

🌢 Guinea pigs: one to two days

🌢 Humans: three days

🌢 Elephants: four days

🌢 Camels: seven months

🌢 Kangaroo rat: ten years, which is almost its entire life!

A prolonged period of unusually low rainfall is called a drought. Droughts can be caused by weather systems, but they can also be caused by climate change. As the world warms up, droughts are becoming more common.

South Africa is one of the world's driest countries and a drought was declared in Cape Town in 2017. The city's taps were on course to run dry and only through careful water conservation did the water shortage come to an end. People were asked to practise water-saving methods, such as having shorter showers and only flushing toilets when necessary. Filling swimming pools and washing cars were banned and there were even competitions to see who could wash their clothes the least!

Water is a precious resource and shouldn't be taken for granted. There are many things we can all do to help conserve water:

💧 Turn the tap off while you brush your teeth. By doing this, one person could save more than 500 litres of water a month!

💧 Take short showers rather than baths. Reducing your shower by one minute could help save as much as 3,500 litres of water per year!

💧 Make sure washing machines and dishwashers are full before putting them on.

💧 Rather than garden hoses, use other ways to water plants. You could suggest installing a water butt in the garden to collect rainwater. Or you could use any leftover water in your drinking glasses and water bottles.

💧 If you notice leaks or dripping taps around the house, make sure you tell someone so they can be fixed.

Emma Beswetherick is the mother of two young children and wanted to write exciting, inspirational and enabling adventure stories to share with them. Emma works in publishing and lives in south-west London with her family and two ragdoll cats, one of whom was the inspiration for Thunder. *The Great Safari Rescue* is her fifth book.

Find her at: emmabeswetherick.com

Anna Woodbine is an independent book designer and illustrator based in the hills near Bath. She works on all sorts of book covers from children's to adult's, classics to crime, memoirs to meditation. She takes her tea with a dash of milk (Earl Grey, always), loves the wind in her face, comfortable shoes and that lovely damp smell after it's rained.

Find her at: thewoodbineworkshop.co.uk

JOIN THE CONVERSATION ONLINE!

Follow us for a behind-the-scenes
look at our books. There'll be exclusive
content and giveaways galore!
You can access learning resources here:
oneworld-publications.com/rtb
Find us on YouTube
as Oneworld Publications
or on Facebook @oneworldpublications
or on Twitter and Instagram as
@Rocktheboatnews